MW01234288

Drought

BY DUNCAN SCHEFF

Raintree Steck-Vaughn Publishers

A Harcourt Company

Austin · New York
www.steck-vaughn.com

Published by Raintree Steck-Vaughn Publishers, an imprint of Steck-Vaughn Company.

Library of Congress Cataloging-in-Publication Data

Drought/by Duncan Scheff.

p.cm.—(Nature on the rampage)

Includes bibliographical references and index.

ISBN 0-7398-4702-3

1. Droughts—Juvenile literature. [1. Droughts.] I. Title. II. Series.

QC929.25 .S33 2001

363.34'926—dc21

2001019864

Printed and bound in the United States of America

1 2 3 4 5 6 7 8 9 10 WZ 05 04 03 02 01

Produced by Compass Books

Photo Acknowledgments

Darrel Plowes, 4, 7, 8, 16, 23, 24, 26, 29

Root Resources/Louise K. Broman, title page; Doug Sherman, 14

Visuals Unlimited/Norris Blake, cover

Content Consultants

Dr. Len Keshishian
State University of New York
Department of Earth Sciences

Maria Kent Rowell
Science Consultant
Sebastopol, California

David Larwa
National Science Education Consultant
Educational Training Services
Brighton, Michigan

This book supports the National Science Standards.

CONTENTS

The water level in this river has dropped because of drought, leaving mud.

WHEN EARTH DRIES

Having no water can be more deadly than having too much **precipitation**. Precipitation means any form of water that falls from the sky, including rain and snow. A long period of unusually dry weather is called a drought. Droughts kill thousands of people each year.

Scientists look at an area's average rainfall to decide whether its dry weather is a drought. Average means the usual amount. For example, 25 inches (63.5 cm) of rain in one year is normal in parts of California, but is a drought in southern Florida. This is because southern Florida usually receives much more rain than certain parts of California.

What Droughts Are Like

Droughts can happen almost anywhere on Earth. Places with average low precipitation are at greater risk than places with average high precipitation. India, eastern China, northern South America, and northern Africa are all in danger of drought. In the United States, droughts are common in Oklahoma, Kansas, and Nebraska.

During a drought, the weather is usually hot. Rain may not fall for weeks, months, or years. The water level falls in rivers, lakes, and ponds. During long droughts, these water supplies may dry up. When that happens, people and animals may not be able to find clean water to drink.

Sometimes it may rain briefly during a drought. But this rain is not enough to keep the soil wet. The water evaporates before it soaks into the soil. To evaporate is to turn from a liquid into a gas. The heat bakes the soil until it dries and cracks. The top of the soil can blow away in the wind.

These crops have dried out and died from a drought.

Droughts are a danger to plants, animals, and people. Plants and crops cannot grow in dry soil. They turn brown and die.

Droughts often create **famines**. A famine is a long period of low food supply. Animals that feed on plants or crops may starve. To starve is to suffer or die from lack of food. People may run out of food if they have no crops or animals to eat.

This dust storm is blowing toward an African town.

What Droughts Do

Long periods of drought may lead to soil **erosion**. Erosion is the slow moving away of something by water or wind. Usually plant roots hold soil in place. But drought often kills all the plants in an area. Without plants, soil becomes loose and dusty. Wind carries away the rich, top layer of soil. New plants cannot grow without this soil.

Sometimes wind picks up soil that has become loose and dusty and creates a dust storm. These storms can be 400 miles (644 km) wide and carry millions of tons of soil, dust, or sand. Winds can whip the loose dust into a swirling black cloud up to 14,000 feet (4,267 m) high.

Deadly dust storms can last for several days. People cannot see more than 400 yards (366 m) ahead of them. The dust can hurt people's eyes, making them blind for a short time. Sometimes people may become sick or suffocate from breathing the dust. To suffocate is to die from lack of air. Up to 15 feet (5 m) of dust may pile up around houses.

During a drought, dust devils may form. These winds spin, creating a circling column of dust. Dust devils are small and do not last for very long.

Fire is another danger during droughts. Dry plants easily catch fire if they are hit by lightning. Hot winds spread the fire until it burns out of control.

WATER VAPOR COOLS

EVAPORATION

CONDENSATION

PRECIPITATION

LAKE

WATER TABLE

This diagram shows how the water cycle works.

ALL ABOUT DROUGHTS

The water cycle can affect droughts. The water cycle is the process that allows Earth to use its water over again.

The cycle begins when water evaporates. Liquid water turns into gas called water vapor. Water vapor rises into the atmosphere. These layers of air surround Earth. When the water vapor meets colder air, it cools and condenses. To condense is to change from a gas into a liquid form. The water vapor combines into tiny drops of water called droplets. These droplets join together to form clouds.

In the clouds, the droplets bump against each other and grow into drops of water heavy enough to fall back to Earth again.

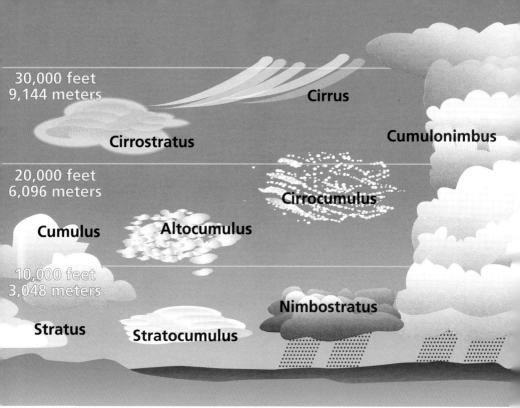

30,000 feet
9,144 meters

Cirrus

Cirrostratus

Cumulonimbus

20,000 feet
6,096 meters

Cirrocumulus

Cumulus

Altocumulus

10,000 feet
3,048 meters

Nimbostratus

Stratus

Stratocumulus

This illustration shows the different kinds of clouds that form in low-pressure areas.

What Causes a Drought?

Scientists are not sure exactly what causes a drought. They believe that several things can affect the start of a drought.

A great deal of water evaporates from the ocean's surface. Warm air over the oceans carries a lot of this water vapor. In some

places, winds usually blow the moist air over land. During a drought, winds may blow the moist air somewhere else.

Sometimes air pressure may affect the water cycle. Air pressure is the weight of the air pressing on the ground. A high-pressure area causes good weather. A low-pressure area can cause clouds to form. A drought occurs when a high-pressure area sits over a place for a long time. The high-pressure area stops warm, moist air from flowing in. If moist air is blocked, there is no water vapor to condense into clouds. No rain will fall until the high-pressure air has moved.

In some areas, changes in climate can cause a drought. The climate is the usual weather of an area over a long time. For example, a small change in the temperature of parts of the ocean can change the way water evaporates. This may then change where warm masses of air form. As the warm air passes over land, rain may fall in different places. Some areas may flood, while others suffer through droughts.

▲ **Farmers irrigate their crops during drought to keep the plants alive.**

Dealing with Drought

People cannot stop droughts from happening. They usually have no idea when a drought will develop. By planning ahead, people can sometimes save enough water to live through a drought.

Reservoirs are one way to fight drought. A reservoir is a holding area for storing large amounts of water. Reservoirs can be natural, such as lakes. People make some reservoirs by building dams on large rivers. A dam is a strong barrier built across a river or stream to hold back water. The water grows deeper behind the dam and forms a lake. People can use the water in a reservoir when drought has taken hold.

Some governments make laws about using water during drought. People cannot fill swimming pools, wash their cars, or water the grass. They may also save water by taking quick showers instead of baths. By doing these things, people save water by using only as much as they need and no more.

During droughts, farmers must **irrigate** or their crops will die. To irrigate is to pipe water to dry land. Farmers use stored water to keep the crops alive. This helps prevent famine from happening.

A drought near the equator has produced the conditions needed for this dust devil to form.

HISTORY AND DROUGHTS

In warm areas near the equator, many areas have a rainy season and a dry season each year. During the rainy season, a great deal of rain falls. People store water for use during the dry season when no rain falls. Droughts happen when not enough rain falls during the rainy season. When this happens, there is no water to use during the dry season.

In India, monsoon winds carry warm, moist air from the Indian Ocean over land. Sometimes the monsoons blow to different places. Then some areas flood, and others do not receive enough rain. This happened in India in 1769 and 1770. A total of more than ten million people died because of the drought.

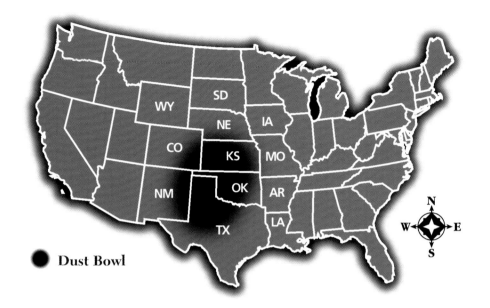

Dust Bowl

This map shows where the American Dust Bowl was in the 1930s.

The American Dust Bowl

One of the worst droughts in U.S. history occurred in the Great Plains during the 1930s. The driest years ever recorded in the area were 1934 and 1936. Millions of people suffered because their crops died.

Soil erosion became worse than usual because there were fewer plant roots to hold soil in place. Strong winds picked up the loose soil and blew it around. There were so many dust storms that the area was called the Dust Bowl. People called the dust storms "black blizzards" because the sky grew dark when they struck.

Farmers could not earn money because their crops would not grow in the dry soil. Thousands of families became poor and homeless. They had no food to eat. Many of these people left the Great Plains to move to the coasts. They wanted to find jobs and places where they could grow food. Oklahoma was one of the hardest hit states. Many people from there moved to California. The homeless people from the Dust Bowl became known as "Okies."

The drought ended in 1940. People in the Great Plains Dust Bowl were able to grow crops once again.

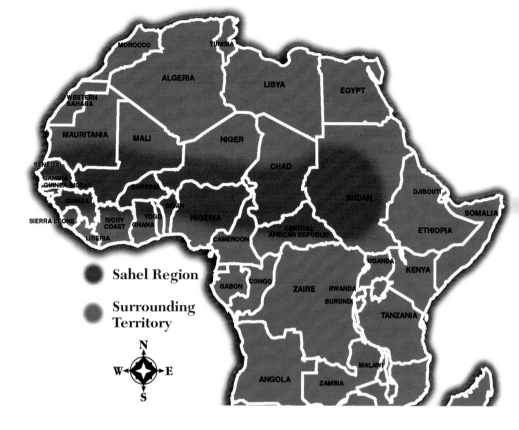

This map shows the semidry Sahel area of Africa. It often suffers from drought.

Drought in the Sahel

Countries in the Sahel area of northern Africa often suffer from drought. This semidry strip of land borders the Sahara Desert. There are many people living in the Sahel. They need water to grow crops for food. They also need water and land to feed their animals. Since it is next to a huge desert, small changes in climate can create a drought. If there are several years of low rainfall, drought could set in.

The Sahel has a rainy season and a dry season. As in India, people in the Sahel need monsoon winds to bring them rain. Deadly droughts begin when the monsoon rains do not come. From 1968 to 1973, rainfall was low or did not come at all. Plants died, and rivers, lakes, and streams dried. Crops did not grow well during these years and little food was stored. More than 200,000 people and about four million animals died during this drought.

During the early 1980s, a deadly Sahel drought happened in Ethiopia. Famine took hold. Millions of people did not have enough food. Countries from around the world sent food to help the Ethiopian people. Even so, about 100,000 people died because of the drought.

Changing Africa

Long and repeated droughts have helped change the land in Africa. Its deserts are spreading. Places that once received heavy rainfall now receive very little. People also cut down native plants and trees to grow crops. These things can cause **desertification**. Desertification is the process where healthy land turns into desert. As more land turns into deserts, people may have to find new places to live.

Savannas are at the greatest risk of desertification. A savanna is grassland with few or no trees. All grasslands are semiarid. Semiarid means that the climate is dry, but not as dry as deserts. Grasslands receive 10 to 50 inches (25 to 127 cm) of rain each year. They usually form on the borders of deserts. Years of farmers growing crops combined with drought have killed many plants that grow in savannas. Soil becomes loose and blows away. Over many years, the savannas turn into deserts.

▲ The sands of the spreading desert have partly buried this house.

Deserts also spread when too many grazing animals are eating grasslands. Grazing animals are grass-eating animals that people raise for food. Soil blows away when too many animals held in one area eat too much of the grass there.

Palmer Drought Severity Index

Precipitation Above or Below Normal	Palmer Classification
4 in. or more 10.16 cm or more	Extremely Wet
3 to 3.99 in. 7.62 to 10.15 cm	Very Wet
2 to 2.99 in. 5.08 to 7.61 cm	Moderately Wet
1 to 1.99 in. 2.54 to 5.07 cm	Slightly Wet
0.99 to -0.99 in. 2.53 to -2.53 cm	Near Normal
-1 to -1.99 in. -2.54 to -5.07 cm	Mild Drought
-2 to -2.99 in. -5.08 to -7.61	Moderate Drought
-3 to -3.99 in -7.62 to -10.15 cm	Severe Drought
-4 in. or less in -10.16 cm or less	Extreme Drought

This is the Palmer Drought Severity Index.

SCIENCE AND DROUGHT

Scientists who study the weather are called **meteorologists**. Some of these scientists search for the causes of droughts. They want to give people early warning about weather changes that may cause droughts. Then people can prepare for future dry weather.

Meteorologists measure the strength of droughts with the Palmer Drought Severity Index. This index compares an area's water need with the precipitation it receives. An index number of 2 to -2 means there is no drought. A number between -2 and -3 means an area has a mild drought. A serious drought receives a number between -3 and -4. Numbers below -4 mean a deadly drought has hit.

▲ This scientist is studying ways to help
keep trees from dying during drought.

Tools

Meteorologists use many tools to help
them study the weather. Weather **satellites**
are spacecraft that circle Earth. They have
scientific instruments on them. Weather
satellites take pictures of clouds and send
them back to Earth. Meteorologists study the

pictures to see where precipitation is forming. Special photographs taken from satellites also show meteorologists how heat is spread around Earth.

Meteorologists who study droughts must study history. They must look at rainfall measurements through history to learn about weather patterns. A pattern is something that repeats itself. By studying history, scientists have found that droughts happen in some places once every seven to ten years.

Scientists sometimes look at tree rings to study the weather of long ago. Trees grow larger each year. As they do, they form a ring in their trunks. Each ring equals one year of growth. Trees grow more during wet years. Rings for these years are wide. During droughts, trees barely grow. Rings for these years are thin. By studying tree rings, scientists learned about a drought from 2,000 years ago. It covered a wide area of the southwestern United States and lasted 26 years.

Droughts in the Future

Most scientists believe that climate data shows that Earth is slowly growing warmer. Global warming is the rising temperatures caused by the greenhouse effect. The greenhouse effect happens when carbon dioxide and moisture mix in the atmosphere. Carbon dioxide is a gas. It is pumped into the air by cars, factories, and burning wood and coal as fuel. The carbon dioxide and water vapor keep some warm air from leaving our atmosphere. This raises the temperatures on Earth. Some scientists **predict** that global warming will change the climate around the world. They think this change could lead to long, deadly droughts.

Other scientists study cloud seeding. They drop special chemicals into clouds. The chemicals sometimes cause rain to form in the clouds. Some scientists believe cloud seeding could help places suffering from drought. Other scientists say that cloud seeding does not really work.

▲ The row of trees around this farm field helps stop soil from blowing away.

People are planting rows of trees around grassland to stop soil from blowing away. Farmers are learning better ways to grow crops. By doing these things, scientists hope to stop famines and keep deserts from spreading. By using water wisely, scientists hope that more people will live through droughts.

GLOSSARY

desertification (de-zur-tuh-fuh-KAY-shuhn)—the process where healthy land turns into desert

erosion (I-ROH-zhuhn)—the slow moving away of soil by water or wind

famine (FAM-uhn)—a serious food shortage that causes starvation and death

irrigate (IHR-uh-gate)—to pipe water to dry land

meteorologist (mee-tee-ur-OL-oh-jist)—a scientist who studies weather

precipitation (pri-sip-i-TAY-shuhn)—forms of water that fall from the sky, including rain, snow, ice, and hail

predict (pri-DIKT)—to make an educated guess about a future event

reservoir (REZ-uh-vwar)—a place where water is collected and stored

satellite (SAT-uh-lite)—a spacecraft with scientific instruments that orbits Earth

INTERNET SITES AND ADDRESSES

National Drought Mitigation Center
http://enso.unl.edu/ndmc/

National Weather Service
http://www.nws.noaa.gov/

NOAA's Drought Information Center
http://www.drought.noaa.gov/

The Weather Dude
http://www.wxdude.com/

American Meteorological Society
45 Beacon Street
Boston, MA   02108-3693

National Drought Mitigation Center
236 L.W. Chase Hall
P.O. Box 830749
University of Nebraska-Lincoln
Lincoln, NE 68583-0749

INDEX